HANDCUFFED FOR BAD BEHAVIOR

Hucow Milking Story

Leandra Camilli

ISBN: 9798840044469
Imprint: Independently published

1st edition

Cover design by: Leandra Camilli

CONTENTS

CHAPTER 1

Not the place where I wanted to be.

Not with these people looking at me.

I mean, I was in the middle of a crowd, but I was still certain that they were looking at me.

Judging me.

Someone was standing on a raised platform and speaking, but I couldn't pay any attention to his words.

I couldn't stop thinking that something had to be wrong with this. All the hucows were women and all the trainers and professors were men.

Obviously, all the hucows were going to be women, but all the teachers were men? What the hell was going on here?

They were keeping us naked in the main hall, and we couldn't do anything about it.

One peep and it would be enough to put us in their cells.

They were cold, unforgiving. I couldn't stand even thinking about those cells, and I was certain that it would never happen to me.

The teachers would never put us in one of those cells.

It didn't matter that they were all smoking hot.

They were never going to make me think that anything could ever happen between us.

Even though...

Even though the reason why I came here was simple.

I thought that I could strike gold by coming here. Thought that one of the teachers would have eyes for me, but that lasted until I realized that they were all married.

And I wasn't lying. All of them had marriage rings on their fingers, destroying all hope that I once had. So why did I even think that coming here was going to solve anything?

The truth was that it wasn't going to solve anything.

We were all here, in the main hall, and the teacher on the raised platform was speaking about what our lives here were going to be like.

It was like time was passing but wasn't at the same time.

I took a deep breath in, closed my eyes, and thought that for sure nothing else was going to happen here.

We were going to be taken to our bedrooms, they were going to lock us in there, and that was going to be it.

I was so certain of that that I wasn't even aware of what was happening around me or what my ears were hearing.

That was why I was so stunned when I noticed someone right by my side, and it wasn't one of the candidates.

It was actually a man. One of the teachers, I noticed right away. He was nothing short of stunning.

He looked just like all the other teachers, but he was also different.

Blond hair.

Stubble on his face.

Square jawline.

Full lips.

A massive, hulky body.

And eyes that looked into mine as though he could read everything I was thinking.

Even though I wasn't even trying to say anything, I felt like I was mumbling. I was so stunned that my body had frozen up. And I was certain that he was aware of the effect he was having on me. It was why he wasn't smiling right now.

Such a devilish, evil smile, and he wasn't ashamed of it.

And I was certain that he knew how aroused he was making me feel, too.

After all, why else would he be pulling up the side of his lips like that, showing me a little of his teeth? Even though I couldn't see much, there was no denying that they were shining.

"Who are you?" I asked, hoping that he was going to be forthcoming with his answer, but knowing that he didn't have to.

He didn't say anything for the first few seconds, making me feel so anxious, and I was certain he was using that to his advantage as well.

If there was something I learned about the teachers here in Deimour College, it was that they had no boundaries when it came to taking advantage of their students.

"I'm Jason. I'm one of the teachers here in the college," he replied, not giving me any new information. Of course he wouldn't.

"I already knew that," I said, my eyes moving up and down while I felt some wetness and heat between my legs. It was impossible not to be feeling that way when he was so hot and was so incredibly close to me.

He was so close that he was making it difficult for me to breathe.

I just couldn't stop scrutinizing every part of his body.

His rippling muscles.

His bulging biceps.

His crotch.

The way his shirt showed off his abs.

And pretty much everything else. The more I looked at this man, Jason, the more I felt absolutely stunned.

And that made me feel like doing something I thought I never would.

Bad behavior.

Behaving in a way that would put me into trouble.

I knew that was a mistake, but I was still willing to go through with it until the end.

But what would be my punishment if that happened?

"Do you want something from me?" I asked and for the time being, it was like everything happening around me didn't matter anymore.

"I don't know. You tell me."

I checked him out from bottom to top again, my eyes lingering on his crotch. I didn't know if he was wearing tight boxer briefs, but his bulge was so big, and it kept on making me think about what it would be like to feel it with my fingers.

Should I do that? I didn't know, and I was soon realizing that I had to make a decision. After all, the other teacher, whose name I didn't know, was already moving away from the raised platform after speaking his lines in front of the students.

We were all going somewhere else, but I realized that I didn't have to.

After all, Jason was with me.

His eyes were staring at me.

"I think you know what I want from you, and I think you also know why you came here."

He was so sure of himself that it was maddening, and it still melted my heart.

Could I really not do what he wanted? The more time passed here, the more I realized that it was impossible not to.

Thus, without giving it a second thought, I just moved away with him somewhere else.

But we weren't going with the other teachers and the students. We were going to a separate room in Deimour College, and I couldn't wait for some sexy time with Jason.

I knew he was unbelievably hung.

CHAPTER 2

I was with Jason in a separate room, and it was dark. I couldn't see much of anything.

Even though it should be making me feel afraid of this, I was having the opposite reaction.

It was turning me on.

It was like that because Jason was right behind me, and I could feel his fingers on my legs.

One interesting thing about this was that he was still clothed. I didn't know what he was thinking, doing this with his clothes still on, but it was getting on my nerves.

I just wanted him to lower his pants and show me how big he was.

A stray thought just crossed my mind, and I didn't know what to do with it.

What if he got me pregnant? What if he knocked me up?

If that happened, my mind would be so dizzy I would probably pass out.

That was why I wasn't thinking about it much.

I could feel him moving his fingers up on my legs, and I knew what he was looking for.

My bundle of nerves.

And I could feel his hot breath on my neck, and I knew he was smelling me. I could also feel his hard cock pressing against my butt, and it sent shivers of excitement in my body.

It was difficult to control myself, but was there even any point in doing that?

Probably not, I thought when I felt his finger touching my bundle of nerves.

My clit.

He rubbed it.

He scratched it.

He did it once and then didn't stop. In fact, he was continuing on doing that. He was relentless, his fingers just rubbing and brushing, his pace increasing.

And I could still feel his hard cock against my butt, and it teased me so much.

When was he finally going to let me put it between my lips?

I didn't know, but my legs were so incredibly dry right now. I just wanted him to shoot his load inside my mouth, and when that happened, I would feel like I was the happiest woman in the world.

"You do realize that if anyone found out about this, you would be punished, right?" He asked, his fingers still doing their work on my clit.

I could also feel his hot breath swirling over my neck still.

My body was so warm I thought I was going to pass out, but thankfully I didn't. It was his fingers and his dick that were still keeping me aware of everything going on here.

"I didn't know anything about that."

"And why not?"

I bit my bottom lip. Should I tell him the truth?

I should.

"I didn't read the contract before signing it."

For a moment, he stopped rubbing my clit, and I wondered if I just made the biggest mistake of my life.

But then, as if to show me how wrong about it I was, he continued on brushing his finger on my bundle of nerves.

"That means you don't know."

"That I don't know about what?"

"That you should be punished for doing this."

"Punished for what? You took me here."

"It's not that simple. I'm here because I meant to be doing this. It's my destiny. But I know that the other teachers would not approve of this."

I felt my breathing stop. The last thing I wanted was to be punished for having pleasure.

And he continued what he was doing up until the point when I thought I was going to come. My moans and groans filled the room, and I knew that it was just the beginning.

He was going to make me reach my orgasm just by scratching my clit with his finger, and that was something that never happened before.

Even when I was pleasuring myself, I needed something extra. That was why I often used my dildo when I wanted to get off.

"You don't make any sense."

"But I do. I make all the sense in the world."

"You are such an asshole."

"And you love it."

I could tell him he was wrong about that, but what would be the point? I knew I would be wrong about it and I didn't want to come out of this moment thinking that I lied to myself.

It wasn't going to happen.

So why did Jason stop so suddenly, now only slightly grazing his finger on my clit?

I didn't know, but I just wanted to punish him for that.

I looked behind my shoulder, finding his smoldering eyes.

"Why did you stop?"

"I don't think you deserve it. Do you? Do you think you deserve to have an orgasm right now?"

I bit my bottom lip. How was I supposed to answer a question such as that one? He put me in such a difficult position.

"I think I do, yeah."

"Are you going to do something for me so that you can prove that?"

"Do something for you? What thing?"

"I think you know what I'm talking about." He took a deep breath, and I felt his lips grazing the nape of my neck. "And I think you know exactly what's going on here."

"I don't know anything. Stop being so hard on me. I'm doing

everything you want."

"Perhaps…" He breathed, smiling devilishly and I could see his teeth gleaming even though it was dark in the room.

And then, he continued to excite my clit with his finger, this time taking this to a completely new level. I knew he was going to make me come.

My breathing was quickening.

My body was getting warmer.

Everything around me was blurring.

And then, it finally happened.

My body started to convulse, his fingers held me close to him, and I could feel that wave of pleasure and bliss slicing my body.

I was sweaty. I was sweating so much that I would need to take a shower after this was over.

And yet, that didn't bother me.

What mattered was that I just had the most incredible, mouthwatering orgasm of my life, and I would never forget it.

So much so that I knew I was already in love with Jason, something that shouldn't happen.

He turned me around slowly.

His hand cupped my chin.

And was looking into my eyes.

I knew he had something important to tell me. Ground-shaking, even.

CHAPTER 3

Jason said he was going to turn me into a hucow. Finally, it was going to happen. My dreams since coming here. Since before getting into Deimour College, to be honest.

The initiation process was difficult.

That test? I didn't even want to think about it ever again.

But it was also kind of… nostalgic, I guessed.

Shouldn't be thinking about that.

I was lying belly-down on the hospital bed, and the doctors and the nurses were working on me.

Feeling me.

Hands pushing, tugging, grazing.

Something being injected into me.

My body transforming.

I was willing. I told everyone that was going to do this, and it was happening. I could feel my butt getting bigger. I could feel the same happening to my breasts, and I just couldn't wait until it was finally over.

And then, just while the doctors and the nurses continued to do their thing, the door to the room opened. My hand was still dizzy, but I could make out who it was coming inside.

Another teacher, of course.

His eyes were smoldering.

For a moment, I thought he was Jason, but then I realized that he was looking at me differently. He was still looking at me as though he was judging me, but it was a different kind of stare.

What I couldn't understand was why he looked like his twin.

Blonde hair, stubble on his face, chest hair, bulging biceps, rippling muscles, and pretty much everything else that connected them.

Even the color of their eyes was the same.

He knew that something happened, and he had come here to make something very clear to me.

What that was, I didn't know, but my body was already shaking slightly just thinking about it.

He approached me and all the doctors moved away. Even the nurses did the same, leaving me completely alone.

I was alone with the teacher and I couldn't help but wonder what his name was. I did look down at his crotch and I noticed that he was hard.

I figured that was something that happened pretty often here. The teachers were always hard because they were all straight and were still young enough for their hormones to be burning hot in them.

His eyes checked me out.

From bottom to top, left to right. I could feel his eyes lingering on my butt. Was he thinking about fucking me? If that were the case, I would certainly do the same thing I did before.

Bad behavior.

He would have to punish me for that, and perhaps that was the reason why he had come here.

"What's your name, miss?" He asked me, putting his finger on my butt, his thumbs pressing on it slightly.

The audacity of this man! He really thought that he could do that without repercussions. Were we nothing more than toys that the professors could play with without anything bad happening to them?

I was certain that was what he was thinking.

I could feel his finger moving between my ass crack, and I shivered.

I looked into his eyes, and I felt afraid.

"It's Marleen. Marleen Cook," I replied.

"That's a beautiful name for a pretty girl like you. What are you doing here?"

His question made no sense. It was obvious what I was doing here. I came here to Deimour College to be transformed, to turn into a hucow, and that was exactly what was happening here.

Even the doctors and the nurses were almost glued to the walls, looking wide-eyed at this.

They had no idea what was happening, and they shouldn't have.

I doubted that even this teacher knew what was going on.

And thinking that, I had something remarkably important to ask him.

"Who are you? What's your name?" I asked, realizing that his shirt didn't have a pin. Most of the teachers had them with their names engraved on them, but not him.

I wondered why that was.

"Do you really want to know my name? Knowing my name comes with some strings attached, and I have no idea if you would like them."

My heart skipped a beat, thinking about his question. What kind of strings were we talking about here?

I didn't know, but I had already made up my mind about it.

"I still want to know your name."

He took a deep breath, replying, "It's Stephen, but that's everything you are going to know about me. I'm also one of the teachers here."

"I already knew that."

After a moment of silence, he said, "Well, after this is over, I want you to come here to this room." He pointed to the map of the college behind him, and I knew which room that was. "I'm going to be waiting for you there."

"What do you want to do with me there?" I asked, a stray thought crossing my mind.

Was this really happening? I had already thought that I had struck gold with Jason, and I never thought that the same would happen again, much less that it was going to be with another smoking-hot teacher.

His finger dove deeper in my asscrack.

He found my butthole.

What was he thinking he was going to do?

I didn't know, but then he immediately pulled his hand back.

It was just a tease. Such a torment it was.

I didn't know what was happening, but after feeling his finger grazing my butthole, I just wanted him inside of me.

I wanted him to take my virginity. My asshole's virginity, to be more precise.

I took a deep breath in.

The doctors and the nurses were going to resume transforming me into a hucow now.

CHAPTER 4

The transformation was finished and I was making my way to that room. What was I thinking I was going to find over there? I didn't know, but my heart was tight just thinking about it.

Not much longer now.

Some steps. Actually, a couple more steps, and I was finally standing behind the door.

It was a massive, heavy door. It complemented the scenery perfectly. Deimour College looked quite old, akin to Hogwarts.

It was the kind of place where it was cold and uninviting, and I didn't want to spend much time here.

But after the transformation, all I knew was that I needed to be expressed. My breasts were so bigger now that the doctors and nurses told me something I would never forget.

I should actually be calling them udders.

That was the right term they used.

Either way, there was no point thinking about that right now. I knocked on the door, and I was waiting for Stephen to either open it or invite me in.

Was he going to do one of those things?

I didn't know, but time was passing and I was beginning to grow desperate.

The last thing I wanted was to think that I had come here and that it was a waste of time.

Just when I was beginning to get anxious, I heard his voice rumbling from the other side of the door.

"Come in, Marleen. I've been waiting for you."

My hand was shaking, but I still managed to turn the knob and open the door. When I was inside the room, he said, "Close the door. I don't want anyone to find out about this, much less Jason."

Jason? So, he knew about him? Were they fighting over me or something like that?

I didn't think that was the case, but if it was, I would feel flattered.

The room was also dark and I couldn't see much. I supposed that was his way of putting me exactly where he wanted me.

He had me where he wanted me.

Completely submissive.

Feeling extremely uncomfortable.

Everything was so cold that I just wanted to feel his fingers on my skin. I knew how warm his body probably was.

Then, he stood up from where he was sitting. He walked until he was behind me, and I could feel his presence even though I couldn't see his face.

But I could see his white, smoldering eyes in the darkness.

They were assessing me and studying this moment.

Then, I felt his fingers on my shoulders. Both of his hands on my shoulders, to be more precise.

Then, he leaned in, his lips so close to my ears that I knew that whatever he had to say to me was going to make me feel ripples of pleasure in my entire body.

"Bend over, Marleen. I know this is what you want."

"What are you going to do?"

"Should I tell you that before the time is right?"

"Before the time is right?"

"Don't act like you don't know what's going on here."

"You are really making me feel so confused."

"Then, just obey everything I have to say. I promise it's not going to hurt much."

I knew I shouldn't do this, but I still decided to obey every single one of his words.

I bent over, my ass jutting up.

I could feel his fingers on it, massaging my asscheeks.

He knew what he was doing. He applied the right amount of pressure in all the right spots, and I could feel my body shivering.

I was already so wet.

Even though it looked like he was going to take my asshole's virginity, I was hoping he was going to follow up on that by taking the V-card of my pussy too.

But I didn't know if he was willing to do that tonight.

It was more than likely that he was going to stretch this moment out for as long as possible.

"Your skin is so warm and soft," he said, bending his body over mine after lowering his pants.

How big was his cock? I didn't know, but I just kept on thinking about that.

Would he let me wrap my fingers around it and see his length for myself? With my own eyes?

I didn't know, but time was passing and nothing was happening.

He was making me feel so incredibly anxious.

Stephen wasted no time, spreading some lube on his hand. On his fingers, and then he used them in my butthole.

Smearing it.

Coating the inside of it.

Rubbing his fingers in there and eliciting moans of pleasure from me.

It was still going to hurt a lot. When he penetrated me with his cock, I knew I would be screaming.

And yet, I couldn't wait until that happened.

When he was done, I knew that he had gotten the result he wanted.

My asshole was all lubed up and ready for him to pierce it.

Question was… Was he going to do that right now? I didn't know, but I knew that he wanted to make this moment so special. After all, there was nothing like taking the virginity of a hucow's asshole, and I was certain he knew that.

So certain that it was no surprise when he only started to

nudge my orifice with his prick.

And then, it happened.

He finally penetrated me all the way, and it was marvelous. I felt so much pain, but also so much pleasure that it more than compensated for it.

CHAPTER 5

He spread me all the way and I couldn't help but wonder what he was thinking. I supposed that it didn't matter. He was happy, smiling broadly as he continued to pound in and out of me.

But 'pound' was too strong of a word to use right now.

He was slow in the beginning. He was taking his time, making me feel every single second of what was happening.

His fingers dug into my skin.

He was holding me so close to him that I knew I couldn't escape even if I wanted to.

His body was already sweaty, and I could hear him huffing behind me.

I could also feel his balls slapping against my butt. It was hurting so much that I was certain that when this was over, I wouldn't be able to walk and sit normally. Not like I used to.

And yet, Stephen didn't hold anything back.

In the meantime, I couldn't help but wonder when I would finally be expressed. I needed to. My breasts were so big and heavy right now.

They were laden with my milk.

Milk lines continued to ooze from them.

I thought I had come here to be disciplined, but that didn't even start to happen yet. I wasn't going to say I was complaining about this, but I thought that I had come here to learn how to be a hucow.

So that I could be sold later.

Stephen didn't stop, assuming a pace that he was comfortable with.

And I wondered what was going to happen next when the door opened. For a moment, I thought that it was one of the teachers that were going to catch us red-handed, but I was right about that only in part.

It was indeed one of the teachers, but he was Jason and not someone else, as I had feared. He was looking at me as though he was judging me for what I was doing. But it made no sense that he was doing that.

After all, it wasn't the first time that I was fucking here in Deimour College.

In fact, it was my second time doing that, and I was loving every minute of it.

In the meantime, Stephen continued holding me close to him. He was holding me so strongly that he was almost hurting me more than his dick was, and that was saying a lot.

He was even bigger now. I never thought that he could feel even bigger inside of me, and it was marvelous.

This was an experience I would never forget.

He looked up, finding Jason.

"Sorry, mate, but Marleen is mine now."

And the way he said that was so possessive and obsessive that I was feeling flattered. I never thought that I would have two smoking-hot teachers lusting so much after me.

My decision to come here was proving to be the right one.

And I noticed that Jason was holding something slightly shiny in his hands.

I didn't want to admit what it was when my eyes identified it.

It was a pair of handcuffs. He was doing nothing more than holding it in his hands, but I knew he was intending on doing something with it.

What that was, I didn't know, but my heart was tight just thinking about it.

He looked into my eyes and I knew he had something so deeply important to say to me.

So much so that it couldn't be delayed.

"I told you about bad behavior before, and I thought that it was enough, but now I see how wrong I was."

He didn't even give me enough time to say anything. He just walked over to me, grabbed both of my hands, and then sealed the handcuffs on my wrists, showing me that my punishment was only starting.

If only he knew how this was making me feel, he wouldn't be so full of himself right now. He would be changing the punishment for something else.

If before I was already wet, now it was even worse.

I was soaking wet. I was so wet that my arousal was dripping from my pussy, joining with the milk that continued to ooze out of my udders.

He was enjoying what he was seeing, and he wanted a taste of it. It was no surprise then when he got down on his knees before me, grabbing both of my udders.

Udders.

Yes.

I remembered the term correctly this time. I didn't know what it was about it, but I felt like I was losing grasp on reality. The way he was holding my udders was so lust-inducing.

I didn't even know what I was doing anymore. All I knew was that he was going to start to milk me, and it was everything I wanted.

He held nothing back when he put one of my teats between his lips.

He looked up, finding my eyes again, and I almost thought that he was going to say something, but he didn't. He just continued to apply pressure with his lips on my teats, drawing out milk.

That was it.

He was milking me. I thought that when I was going to be expressed that it was going to be a machine doing the job, but it was so different. Something different. Something much better.

And he was relentless as he continued to milk me.

His lips were so warm I just couldn't stop savoring this

moment.

In the meantime, the guy behind me continued to fuck me, and he was also so relentless there was no stopping him. I knew it so well that he was going to come into my rectum.

And I was just waiting for that to happen.

And when it did, I also came at the same time. My body started to shake, but I didn't lose my balance. His fingers continued to hold me so close to him. And he even stopped rolling his hips, jamming his prick all the way inside of me.

He was telling me something important by doing that.

He didn't want me to waste as much as a single drop of his milk, and that for certain was going to happen.

But even after that was over, it still left something that I needed to do. That I wanted to do.

I wanted them both coming inside of me. Knocking me up. And I couldn't wait until that happened.

Now that I was finally regaining some of my grasp on reality, I knew that was exactly what they were going to do.

After all, their stares were more than evident about that.

EPILOGUE

"Oh gosh, she's so tight, isn't she?" Someone that was behind Jason asked, and he spooked me. I didn't think there was anyone behind Jason. He just entered the room and I noticed that he was very similar to Stephen and Jason.

So similar it was almost like he was a twin.

His eyes were staring at me. He was almost making me feel uncomfortable, and I certainly would be feeling that way if it wasn't for the overflowing pleasure in my body.

And looking down, I noticed that he was holding his prick in his fingers.

It was so big. So massive. So heavy and he was oozing pre-come, making me wonder if he was going to let me have a taste of it.

His eyes found Stephen and Jason, and I couldn't help but wonder what was going on in his mind.

As if he could read what I was thinking, he asked, "Can I join?"

Jason and Stephen looked at each other. Were they going to say anything? I didn't know, but what I hated about this moment was that everything stopped. Stephen wasn't fucking me from behind anymore and Jason wasn't sucking my milk.

What was going on?

Then, they nodded. It was almost like they really could read what I was thinking.

"What's your name?" I asked, my eyes diverting to the right as I noticed that he also didn't have a pin on his shirt. How curious.

The longer this was going on, the more I felt so weird, as if I was in a dream.

"It's Ted," he responded, coming toward me. His prick was now right in front of my face, and I couldn't help but wonder if he was going to let me suck him off.

If that happened, it would be like a dream come true.

His eyes locked with mine and he said, "There's only one thing you're meant to do here and that's pleasing us. You really thought that you had come here to learn how to be a hucow? Well, then allow me to tell you that things aren't exactly going to happen that way."

How come it wasn't? The more I was thinking about this, the less it made sense.

But I wasn't going to complain about anything. I was just so overjoyed that they were all doing these incredible things to me.

Pounding in and out of my asshole.

Draining me of my milk.

And now allowing me to suck a dick as massive as his.

It was like I was in heaven, and I was certainly going to cherish every moment of this.

He took a step forward and inserted his prick between my lips, stretching my mouth as wide as it would go.

And further inside it went, touching the back of my throat. My gad reflexes kicked in and I wasn't going to deny it. I thought that I had made the biggest mistake of my life, but things weren't that simple.

In the meantime, Jason continued draining me of my milk.

Slurping sounds bounced in the room.

And Stephen didn't hold anything back, coming in my rectum a second time. I could feel his hot, thick creamy ropes in there a second time. The only pity I was feeling about this was that he didn't knock me up.

I just wished that I wasn't handcuffed, but I wasn't going to complain about that as well.

I was having difficulty breathing, but it was okay. It wasn't like it was the first time it was happening.

I took a deep breath in and looked up, this time finding Ted in front of me again, and I knew he had a plan too dirty to tell me. Not with words, anyway.

He was actually planning on knocking me up, and I couldn't wait until that happened.

My pussy was begging for it.

It was so wet that it had never been this wet before.

And it shone under the light coming from the doorway.

"I'm going to put a baby in your belly. Ready?" He asked, but I was just so tired and spent that I couldn't answer his question. And I was certain that he had planned for that to happen.

Jason and Stephen moved away from me. I didn't think that they felt submissive to Ted, but it was more than obvious that he was going to be the one to take my virginity.

That thought made me feel ripples of pleasure in my body.

He grabbed both of my legs, pulling me to him until my pussy was nudging against his dick. And then, he did it. He was like a lance doing it, impaling me so certainly that I couldn't do anything about it.

And he punched through my hymen as though it was nothing.

I didn't think that it was going to be so rewarding.

I shut my eyes tight and didn't want to open them for anything.

I let my orgasm come and wash over me, making my head dizzy. I really thought that I was going to pass out, but thankfully it didn't happen. Then, he was shooting his load, one hot rope after the other inside of me, knocking me up.

I just never thought that anyone here would do that, and especially that it would happen when I was handcuffed.

And then, looking around me, I knew that it was now Jason's and Stephen's turn. And the best thing about it? It was that they didn't feel like fighting against each other over me.

They could share me.

Everything was fine.

The End

Thank you for reading this story, and you should leave your review. Your feedback helps me immensely!

TEASER: CONDEMNED TO THE HUCOW PRISON

Steamy Milking Story

"The way I see it, Princess, this is your only option," the lawyer sitting across the desk told me. The way Charles was looking at me, it was obvious that he was genuine about his words. My only option. To go to the Hucow Prison, where I didn't know how much my life was going to change. And I was already thinking about it that way, with that level of certainty, mostly because I knew I was going to go there and take that route.

I let out a cloud of breath, feeling it moving over my breasts. There was no denying that they were round and big, something that was already making the lawyer steal glances down at them whenever he could.

And given that I kept on looking down pretty much all the time, feeling so completely ashamed of myself, he had many opportunities to do that.

"I still don't like it."

Charles put the papers down on the desk. Even though he wore a dark suit and it hid most of his body, there was no denying that he was a sight for sore eyes. The stubble on his face, his nose, his plump lips, the harsh cheekbones, and pretty much everything else were making me feel a little hint of lust in me. I couldn't help but wonder what he was like when he was naked after taking a shower.

I imagined Charles walking out of his bathroom with only a towel covering his body. Or maybe he lived alone and he would step out of the bathroom without even that covering him. The thought alone was enough to make me feel slightly wet, and I suddenly found myself rubbing my legs together.

"You don't have to like it, but there is something I can do to make your time there less hard on you," he proposed and I lifted my eyes up. I was still looking down at my legs before that, but now that he was giving me some hope, I wanted to know everything about it.

I noticed him letting out a shadow of breath, his eyes studying me and sizing me up.

And... It was such a pity that I was finally noticing that he had a marriage ring on his finger. I didn't know he was taken, and it was already making me shake my head in complete disappointment.

The worst thing was remembering that I was still a virgin and that I didn't think that that was going to change anytime soon.

"What is it that I can do?" I asked and Charles stood up slowly. I watched carefully as he did that. There was something about the way he moved his body, how tall he was, the shape of his muscles, his confident posture, and pretty much everything else that made me want him completely.

"I'm not sure I should say it." Charles took another deep breath and then stepped over to the window. It overlooked a huge, impressive garden, and even though I was in love with it when I first came here, I didn't have enough time to study it. I wanted to explore it, to feel what it was like to be with those bushes and small trees, but I had something much more important to do here. Not to mention that I was pretty sure the police would not have let me go there, in the first place, without making a fuss about it, and

I didn't want to go through that hassle.

I was checking his behind carefully and slowly. Since stepping into his office, it was the first time that I was having this opportunity. And Charles didn't stop before putting his hand inside his pocket and lighting up a cigarette. Even though I didn't like the smell of the smoke, the fact that he was smoking was making him look even more appetizing than before. I was trying to control it, but it was impossible. My mouth was salivating. I could feel the slow buildup of saliva in it.

I stood up slowly as well. I felt like I needed to be closer to that man as much as possible. Not to mention that I had this strong urge to rip the clothes off his body, and something about the way he was talking right now was telling me that he just might be thinking the same...

SIMILAR BOOKS

SERIES - FERTILE PLAYTHING

1. Condemned to the Hucow Prison

2. Shared at the Hucow Prison

3. Passed Around at the Hucow Prison

4. Chained Up at the Hucow Prison

5. Examined at the Hucow Prison
6. Locked Up in the Hucow Prison

SERIES - FERTILE ONLY

1. Bumping the Teacher

2. Bumping the Midwife

3. Bumping the Farmhand

4. Bumping the Sinner

ABOUT THE AUTHOR

Leandra Camilli's obsession? Writing dirty, steamy stories that make her readers drool. She loves her Alpha males, hucows, sissies, and futas. If you're looking for those kinds of books, look no further.

With a cup of coffee on her table and warm socks on, she writes almost every day. Leandra Camilli has featured in several top 100 categories in the store, and she publishes weekly.

www.ingramcontent.com/pod-product-compliance
Lightning Source LLC
Chambersburg PA
CBHW051939150726
47999CB00006B/2291